KU-256-383

THE ANGELS WEEP

BOOKS BY
WILBUR SMITH

When the Lion Feeds
The Sound of Thunder
The Dark of the Sun
Shout at the Devil
Gold Mine
The Diamond Hunters
The Sunbird
Eagle in the Sky
The Eye of the Tiger
Cry Wolf
A Sparrow Falls
Hungry as the Sea
Wild Justice
A Falcon Flies
Men of Men
The Angels Weep

The Angels Weep

WILBUR SMITH

BOOK CLUB ASSOCIATES LONDON

This edition published 1982 by
Book Club Associates
By arrangement with William Heinemann Ltd.

© Wilbur Smith 1982

Printed in Great Britain by
Richard Clay (The Chaucer Press) Ltd,
Bungay, Suffolk

This book is for my beloved wife
DANIELLE ANTOINETTE

But man, proud man,
Dress'd in a little brief authority,
Most ignorant of what he's most assur'd,
His glassy essence, like an angry ape,
Plays such fantastic tricks before high heaven
As make the angels weep.

Measure for Measure
William Shakespeare

Part One

1895

THREE HORSEMEN rode out from the edge of the forest with a restrained eagerness that not even weary weeks of constant searching could dull.

They reined in, stirrup to stirrup, and looked down into another shallow valley. Each stalk of the dry winter grass bore a fluffy seedhead of a lovely pale rose colour, and the light breeze stirred them and made them dance, so that the herd of sable antelope in the gut of the valley seemed to float belly-deep in a bank of swirling pink mist.

There was a single herd bull. He stood almost fourteen hands tall at the withers. His satiny back and shoulders were black as a panther's, but his belly and the intricate designs of his face-mask were the startling iridescent white of mother-of-pearl. His great ridged horns, curved like Saladin's scimitar, swept back to touch his croup, and his neck was proudly arched as that of a blood Arabian stallion. Long ago hunted to extinction in his former southern ranges, this noblest of all the antelopes of Africa had come to symbolize for Ralph Ballantyne this wild and beautiful new land between the Limpopo and the wide green Zambezi rivers.

The great black bull stared arrogantly at the horsemen on the ridge above him, then snorted and tossed his warlike head. Thick dark mane flying, sharp hooves clattering over the stony ground, he led his chocolate-coloured brood mares at a gallop up and over the far ridge, leaving the watching men mute at their grandeur and their beauty.

Ralph Ballantyne was first to rouse himself and he turned in the saddle towards his father.

'Well, Papa,' he asked, 'do you recognize any landmarks?'

'It was more than thirty years ago,' Zouga Ballantyne murmured, a little frown of concentration puckering an arrowhead in the centre of his forehead, 'thirty years, and I was riddled with malaria.' Then he turned to the third rider, the little wizened Hottentot, his companion and servant since those far-off days. 'What do you think, Jan Cheroot?'

The Hottentot lifted the battered regimental cap from his head, and smoothed the little peppercorns of pure white wool that covered his scalp. 'Perhaps—'

Ralph cut in brusquely, 'Perhaps it was all merely a fever dream.'

The frown on his father's handsome bearded features sharpened, and the scar upon his cheek flushed from bone-porcelain to rose, while Jan Cheroot grinned with anticipation; when these two were together it was better entertainment than a cock-fight any day.

'Damn it, boy,' Zouga snapped. 'Why don't you go back to the wagons and keep the women company.' Zouga drew the thin chain from his fob pocket and dangled it before his son's face. 'There it is,' he snapped, 'that's the proof.'

On the ring of the chain hung a small bunch of keys, and other oddments, a gold seal, a St Christopher, a cigar-cutter and an irregular lump of quartz the size of a ripe grape. This last was mottled like fine blue marble and starred through its centre with a thick wedge of gleaming native metal.

'Raw red gold,' said Zouga. 'Ripe for the picking!'

Ralph grinned at his father, but it was an insolent and provocative grin, for he was bored. Weeks of wandering and fruitless searching were not Ralph's style at all.

'I always suspected that you picked that up from a pedlar's stall on the Grand Parade at Cape Town, and that it's only fool's gold anyway.'

The scar on his father's cheek turned a darker furious red, and Ralph laughed delightedly and clasped Zouga's shoulder.

'Oh, Papa, if I truly believed that, do you think I would waste weeks of my time? What with the railroad building and the dozen other balls I am juggling, would I be here, instead of in Johannesburg or Kimberley?'

He shook Zouga's shoulder gently, the smile no longer mocking. 'It's here – we both know it. We could be standing on the reef at this very moment, or it could be just over the next ridge.'

Slowly the heat went out of Zouga's scar, and Ralph went on evenly, 'The trick, of course, is to find it again. We could stumble over it in the next hour, or search another ten years.'

Watching father and son, Jan Cheroot felt a small prick of disappointment. He had seen them fight once before, but that was long ago. Ralph was now in the full prime of his manhood, almost thirty years of age, accustomed to handling the hundreds of rough men that he employed in his transport company and his construction teams, handling them with tongue and boot and fist. He was big and hard and strutty as a game cock, but Jan Cheroot suspected that

10

the old dog would still be able to roll the puppy in the dust. The praise name that the Matabele had given Zouga Ballantyne was 'Bakela', the Fist, and he was still fast and lean. Yes, Jan Cheroot decided regretfully, it would still be worth watching, but perhaps another day, for already the flare of tempers had faded and the two men were again talking quietly and eagerly, leaning from their saddles towards each other. Now they seemed more like brothers, for although the family resemblance was unmistakable, yet Zouga did not seem old enough to be Ralph's father. His skin was too clear and unlined, his eye too quick and vital and the faint lacing of silver in his golden beard might have been merely the bleaching of the fierce African sun.

'If only you had been able to get a sun-sight, the other observations you made were all so accurate,' Ralph lamented. 'I was able to go directly to every cache of ivory that you left that year.'

'By that time the rains had started,' Zouga shook his head, 'and, by God, how it rained! We hadn't seen the sun for a week, every river was in full spate, so we were marching in circles, trying to find a ford—' he broke off, and lifted the reins in his left hand. 'But I've told the tale a hundred times. Let's get on with the search,' he suggested quietly, and they trotted down off the ridge into the valley, Zouga stooping from the saddle to examine the ground for chips of broken reef, or swivelling slowly to survey the skyline to try and recognize the shape of the crests or the blue loom of a distant kopje against the towering African sky, where the silver fair-weather cumulus sailed high and serene.

'The only definite landmark we have to work on is the site of the ruins of Great Zimbabwe,' Zouga muttered. 'We marched eight days due westwards from the ruins.'

'Nine days,' Jan Cheroot corrected him. 'You lost one day when Matthew died. You were in fever. I had to nurse you like a baby, and we were carrying that damned stone bird.'

'We couldn't have made good more than ten miles a day.' Zouga ignored him. 'Eight days' march, not more than eighty miles.'

'And Great Zimbabwe is there. Due east of us now.' Ralph reined in his horse as they came out on the next ridge. 'That is the Sentinel.' He pointed at a rocky kopje, the distant blue summit shaped like a crouching lion. 'The ruins are just beyond, I would never mistake that view.'

For both father and son the ruined city had a special significance. There within the massive stone-built walls Zouga and Jan Cheroot had found the ancient graven bird images that had been abandoned

11

by the long-vanished inhabitants. Despite the desperate straits to which they had been reduced by fever and the other hardships of the long expedition from the Zambezi river in the north, Zouga had insisted on carrying away with him one of the statues.

Then many years later it had been Ralph's turn. Guided by his father's diary and the meticulous sextant observations that it contained, Ralph had once again won through to the deserted citadel. Though he had been pursued by the border impis of Lobengula, the Matabele king, he had defied the king's taboo on the holy place and had spirited away the remaining statues. Thus all three men had intimate knowledge of those haunting and haunted ruins, and as they stared at the far hills that marked the site, they were silent with their memories.

'I still wonder, who were the men who built Zimbabwe?' Ralph asked at last. 'And what happened to them?' There was an uncharacteristic dreamy tone to his voice, and he expected no answer. 'Were they the Queen of Sheba's miners? Was this the Ophir of the Bible? Did they carry the gold they mined to Solomon?'

'Perhaps we will never know.' Zouga roused himself. 'But we do know they valued gold as we do. I found gold foil and beads and bars of bullion in the courtyard of Great Zimbabwe, and it must be within a few miles of where we stand that Jan Cheroot and I explored the shafts that they drove into the earth, and found the broken reef piled in dumps ready for crushing.' Zouga glanced across at the little Hottentot. 'Do you recognize any of this?'

The dark pixie face wrinkled up like a sun-dried prune as Jan Cheroot considered. 'Perhaps from the next ridge,' he muttered lugubriously, and the trio rode down into the valley that looked like a hundred others they had crossed in the preceding weeks.

Ralph was a dozen strides ahead of the others, cantering easily, swinging his mount to skirt a thicket of the dense wild ebony, when abruptly he stood in the stirrups, snatched his hat from his head and waved it high.

'Tally ho!' he yelled. 'Gone away!'

And Zouga saw the burnt gold flash of fluid movement across the far slope of open ground.

'Three of the devils!' Ralph's excitement and his loathing was clear in the pitch and timbre of his voice. 'Jan Cheroot, you turn 'em on the left! Papa, stop them crossing the ravine!'

The easy manner of command came naturally to Ralph Ballantyne, and the two older men accepted it as naturally, while none of them questioned for an instant why they should destroy the magnificent animals that Ralph had flushed from the ebony thicket. Ralph owned two hundred wagons, each drawn by sixteen draught oxen. King's Lynn, Zouga's estates, taken up with the land grants that the British South Africa Company had issued to the volunteers who had destroyed the Matabele king's impis, covered many tens of thousands of acres that were stocked with the pick of the captured Matabele breeding herds running with blood bulls imported from Good Hope and old England.

Father and son were both cattlemen, and they had suffered the terrible depredations of the lion prides which infested this lovely land north of the Limpopo and Shashi rivers. Too often they had heard their valuable and beloved beasts bellowing in agony in the night, and in the dawn found their ravaged carcasses. To both of them, lions were the worst kind of vermin, and they were elated with this rare chance of taking a pride in broad daylight.

Ralph yanked the repeating Winchester rifle from the leather scabbard under his left knee, as he urged the chestnut gelding into full gallop after the big yellow cats. The lion had been the first away, and Ralph had only a glimpse of him, sway-backed and swing-bellied, the dense dark ruff of his mane fluffed out with alarm, padding majestically on heavy paws into the scrub. The older lioness followed him swiftly. She was lean and scarred from a thousand hunts, blue with age across the shoulders and back. She went away at a bounding gallop. However, the younger lioness, unaccustomed to men, was bold and curious as a cat. She was still faintly cub-spotted across her creamy gold belly, and she turned on the edge of the thicket to snarl at the pursuing horseman. Her ears lay flat against her skull, her furry pink tongue curled out over her fangs, and her whiskers were white and stiff as porcupine quills.

Ralph dropped his reins onto the gelding's neck, and the horse responded instantly by plunging to a dead stop and freezing for the shot, only the scissoring of his ears betraying his agitation.

Ralph tossed up the Winchester and fired as the buttplate slapped into his shoulder. The lioness grunted explosively as the bullet thumped into her shoulder, angled for the heart. She went up in a high sunfishing somersault, roaring in her death frenzy. She fell and rolled on her back, tearing at the scrub with fully extended yellow claws, and then stretching out in a last shuddering convulsion before slumping into the softness of death.

Ralph pumped a fresh round into the chamber of the Winchester, and gathered up the reins. The gelding leaped forward.

Out on the right Zouga was pounding up the lip of the ravine, leaning forward in the saddle, and at that moment the second lioness broke into the open ahead of him, going for the deep brush-choked ravine at a driving run, and Zouga fired still at full gallop. Ralph saw dust spurt under the animal's belly.

'Low and left. Papa is getting old,' Ralph thought derisively, and brought the gelding crashing down to a stiff-legged halt. Before he could fire, Zouga had shot again, and the lioness collapsed and rolled like a yellow ball on the stony earth, shot through the neck a hand's span behind the ear.

'Bully for you!' Ralph laughed with excitement, and kicked his heels into the gelding's flank as they charged up the slope, shoulder to shoulder.

'Where is Jan Cheroot?' Zouga shouted, and as if in reply they heard the clap of rifle fire in the forest on the left, and they swung the horses in that direction.

'Can you see him?' Ralph called.

The bush was thicker ahead of them, and the thorn branches whipped at their thighs as they passed. There was a second shot, and immediately afterwards the furious ear-numbing roars of the lion mingled with Jan Cheroot's shrill squeals of terror.

'He is in trouble!' Zouga called anxiously, as they burst out of the thick scrub.

Before them there lay parkland, fine open grass beneath the tall flat-topped acacia trees along the crest of the ridge. A hundred yards ahead Jan Cheroot was tearing along the crest, twisted in the saddle to look over his shoulder, his face a mask of terror, his eyes huge and glistening white. He had lost his hat and rifle, but he was lashing his mount across the neck and shoulders, although the animal was already at a wild uncontrolled gallop.

The lion was a dozen strides behind them, but gaining with each elastic bound as though they were standing still. Its heaving flank was painted slick and shiny with bright new blood, shot through the guts, but the wound had not crippled nor even slowed the beast. Rather it had maddened him, so that the solid blasts of sound from his throat sounded like the thunder of the skies.

Ralph swerved his gelding to try and intercept the little Hottentot, and alter the angle to give himself an open shot at the lion, but at that moment the cat came up out of its flat snaking charge, reared up over the bunched and straining quarters of the horse and raked them with long curved talons so that the sweat-darkened hide opened in deep parallel wounds, and the blood smoked from them in a fine crimson cloud.

14

The horse shrieked and lashed out with its hind hooves, catching the lion in his chest, so that he reeled and lost a stride. Immediately he gathered himself and came again, quartering in beside the running horse, his eyes inscrutably yellow as he prepared to leap astride the panic-driven animal.

'Jump, Jan Cheroot!' Ralph yelled. The lion was too close to risk a shot. 'Jump, damn you!' But Jan Cheroot did not appear to have heard him, he was clinging helplessly to the tangled flying mane, paralysed with fear.

The lion rose lightly into the air, and settled like a huge yellow bird on the horse's back, crushing Jan Cheroot beneath his massive, blood-streaked body. At that instant, horse and rider and lion seemed to disappear into the very earth, and there was only a swirling column of dust to mark where they had been. Yet the shattering roars of the enraged animal and Jan Cheroot's howls of terror grew even louder as Ralph galloped up to the point on the ridge where they had disappeared.

With the Winchester in one hand he kicked his feet from the stirrup irons and jumped from the saddle, letting his own momentum throw him forward until he stood on the edge of a sheer-sided pitfall at the bottom of which lay a tangle of heaving bodies.

'The devil is killing me!' screamed Jan Cheroot, and Ralph could see him pinned beneath the body of the horse. The horse must have broken its neck in the fall, it was a lifeless heap with head twisted up under its shoulder and the lion was ripping the carcass and saddle, trying to reach Jan Cheroot.

'Lie still,' Ralph shouted down at him. 'Give me a clear shot!'

But it was the lion that heard him. He left the horse and came up the vertical side of the pit with the ease of a cat climbing a tree, his glossy muscular hindquarters driving him lightly upwards and his pale yellow eyes fastened upon Ralph as he stood on the lip of the deep hole.

Ralph dropped on one knee to steady himself for the shot, and aimed down into the broad golden chest. The jaws were wide open, the fangs long as a man's forefinger and white as polished ivory, the deafening clamour from the open throat dinned into Ralph's face. He could smell the rotten-flesh taint of the lion's breath and flecks of hot saliva splattered against his cheeks and forehead.

He fired, and pumped the loading-handle and fired again, so swiftly that the shots were a continuous blast of sound. The lion arched backwards, hung for a long moment from the wall of the pit, and then toppled and fell back upon the dead horse.

15

Now there was no movement from the bottom of the pit, and the silence was more intense than the shattering uproar that had preceded it.

'Jan Cheroot, are you all right?' Ralph called anxiously.

There was no sign of the little Hottentot, he was completely smothered by the carcasses of horse and lion.

'Jan Cheroot, can you hear me?'

The reply was in a hollow, sepulchral whisper. 'Dead men cannot hear – it's all over, they have got old Jan Cheroot at last.'

'Come out from under there,' Zouga Ballantyne ordered, as he stepped up to Ralph's shoulder. 'This is no time to play the clown, Jan Cheroot.'

* * *

Ralph dropped a coil of manilla rope down to Jan Cheroot, and between them they hauled him and the saddle from the dead horse to the surface.

The excavation into which Jan Cheroot had fallen was a deep narrow trench along the crest of the ridge. In places it was twenty feet deep, but never more than six feet wide. Mostly it was choked with creepers and rank vegetation, but this could not disguise the certainty that it had been dug by men.

'The reef was exposed along this line,' Zouga guessed, as they followed the edge of the old trench, 'the ancient miners simply dug it out and did not bother to refill.'

'How did they blast the reef?' Ralph demanded. 'That's solid rock down there.'

'They probably built fires upon it, and then quenched it with water. The contraction cracked the rock.'

'Well, they seem to have taken out every grain of the ore body and left nary a speck for us.'

Zouga nodded. 'They would have worked out this section first, and then when the reef pinched out they would have started sinking potholes along the strike to try and intercept it again.' Zouga turned to Jan Cheroot and demanded, 'Now do you recognize this place, Jan Cheroot?' And when the Hottentot hesitated, he pointed down the slope. 'The swamp in the valley down there, and the teak trees—'

'Yes, yes.' Jan Cheroot clapped his hands, and his eyes twinkled with delight. 'This is the same place where you killed the bull elephant – the tusks are on the stoep at King's Lynn.'

16

'The ancient dump will be just ahead.' Zouga hurried forward.

He found the low mound covered by grass, and Zouga went down on his knees to scrabble amongst the grass roots, picking out the chips of white sugar quartz, examining each one swiftly and discarding it. Occasionally he wet one with his tongue, held it to the sunlight to try and highlight the sparkle of metal, then frowned and shook his head with disappointment.

At last he stood and wiped his hands on his breeches.

'It's quartz all right, but the ancient miners must have handsorted this dump. We will have to find the old shafts if we want to see visible gold in the ore.'

From the top of the ancient dump Zouga orientated himself rapidly.

'The carcass of the bull elephant fell about there,' he pointed, and to confirm it Jan Cheroot searched in the grass and lifted a huge thighbone, dry and white as chalk, and at last after thirty years beginning to crumble.

'He was the father of all elephant,' Jan Cheroot said reverently. 'There will never be another like him, and it was he that led us to this place. When you shot him he fell here to mark it for us.'

Zouga turned a quarter-circle and pointed again. 'The ancient shaft where we buried old Matthew will be there.'

Ralph recalled the elephant hunt as his father had described it in his celebrated book *A Hunter's Odyssey*. The black gunbearer had not flinched from the great bull elephant's charge, but had stood it down and handed Zouga the second gun, sacrificing his own life for that of his master. So Ralph understood and remained silent, as Zouga went down on one knee beside the rock pile that marked the gunbearer's grave.

After a minute, Zouga rose and dusted off his knee, and said simply, 'He was a good man.'

'Good, but stupid,' Jan Cheroot agreed, 'a wise man would have run.'

'And a wise man would have chosen a better grave,' Ralph murmured. 'He is plumb in the centre of a gold reef. We will have to dig him out.'

But Zouga frowned. 'Let him lie. There are other shafts along the strike.' He turned away, and the others followed him. A hundred yards farther on, Zouga stopped again. 'Here!' he called with satisfaction. 'The second shaft – there were four of them altogether.'

This opening had also been refilled with chunks of native rock. Ralph shrugged off his jacket, propped his rifle against the bole of

17

the nearest tree and climbed down into the shallow depression until he stooped over the narrow blocked entrance.

'I'm going to open it up.'

They worked for half an hour, prising loose the boulders with a branch of a leadwood and manhandling them aside until they had exposed the square opening to the shaft. It was narrow, so narrow that only a child could have passed through it. They knelt and peered down into it. There was no telling how deep it was, for it was impenetrably black in the depths and it stank of damp, of fungus and bats, and of rotting things.

Ralph and Zouga stared into the opening with a horrid fascination.

'They say the ancients used child slaves or captured Bushmen in the workings,' Zouga murmured.

'We have to know if the reef is down there,' Ralph whispered. 'But no grown man—' he broke off and there was another moment of thoughtful silence, before Zouga and Ralph glanced at each other and smiled, and then both their heads turned in unison towards Jan Cheroot.

'Never!' said the little Hottentot fiercely. 'I am a sick old man. Never! You will have to kill me first!'

* * * *

Ralph found a stump of candle in his saddle-bag, while Zouga swiftly spliced together the three coils of rope used for tethering the horses, and Jan Cheroot watched their preparation like a condemned man watching the construction of the gallows.

'For twenty-nine years, since the day I was born, you have been telling me of your courage and daring,' Ralph reminded him, as he placed an arm around Jan Cheroot's shoulder and led him gently back to the mouth of the shaft.

'Perhaps I exaggerated a little,' Jan Cheroot admitted, as Zouga knotted the rope under his armpits and strapped a saddlebag around his tiny waist.

'You, who have fought wild men and hunted elephant and lion – what can you fear in this little hole? A few snakes, a little darkness, the ghosts of dead men, that's all.'

'Perhaps I exaggerated more than a little,' Jan Cheroot whispered huskily.

'You are not a coward are you, Jan Cheroot?'

'Yes,' Jan Cheroot nodded fervently. 'That is exactly what I am, and this is no place for a coward.'

Ralph drew him back, struggling like a hooked catfish on the end of the rope, lifted him easily and lowered him into the shaft. His protests faded gradually as Ralph paid out the rope.

Ralph was measuring the rope across the reach of his outstretched arms. Reckoning each span at six feet, he had lowered the little Hottentot a little under sixty feet before the rope went slack.

'Jan Cheroot!' Zouga bellowed down the shaft.

'A little cave.' Jan Cheroot's voice was muffled and distorted by echoes. 'I can just stand. The reef is black with soot.'

'Cooking fires. The slaves would have been kept down there,' Zouga guessed, 'never seeing the light of day again until they died.' Then he raised his voice. 'What else?'

'Ropes, plaited grass ropes, and buckets, leather buckets like we used on the diamond diggings at New Rush—' Jan Cheroot broke off with an exclamation. 'They fall to pieces when I touch them, just dust now.' Faintly they could hear Jan Cheroot sneezing and coughing in the dust he had raised and his voice was thickened and nasal as he went on, 'Iron tools, something like an adze,' and when he called again they could hear the tremor in his voice. 'Name of the great snake, there are dead men here, dead men's bones. I am coming up – pull me up!'

Staring down the narrow shaft, Ralph could see the light of the candle flame wavering and trembling at the bottom.

'Jan Cheroot, is there a tunnel leading off from the cave?'

'Pull me up.'

'Can you see a tunnel?'

'Yes, now will you pull me up?'

'Not until you follow the tunnel to the end.'

'Are you mad! I would have to crawl on hands and knees.'

'Take one of the iron tools with you, to break a piece off the reef.'

'No. That is enough. I go no farther, not with dead men guarding this place.'

'Very well,' Ralph bellowed into the hole, 'then I will throw the end of the rope down on top of you.'

'You would not do that!'

'After that I will put the rocks back over the entrance.'

'I am going.' Jan Cheroot's voice had a desperate edge, and once again the rope began slithering down into the shaft like a serpent into its nest.

Ralph and Zouga squatted beside the shaft, passing their last cheroot back and forth and waiting with ill grace and impatience.

'When they deserted these workings, they must have sealed the slaves in the shaft. A slave was a valuable chattel, so that proves they were still working the reef and that they left in great haste.' Zouga paused, cocked his head to listen and then said, 'Ah!' with satisfaction. From the depths of the earth at their feet came the distant clank of metal tool on living rock. 'Jan Cheroot has reached the working-face.'

However, it was many minutes more before they saw the wavering candle light in the bottom of the pit again and Jan Cheroot's pleas, quavering and pitiful, came up to them.

'Please, Master Ralph, I have done it. Now will you pull me up, please?'

Ralph stood with one booted foot on each side of the shaft, and hauled in the rope hand over hand. The muscles of his arms bulged and subsided under the sleeves of his thin cotton shirt, as he lifted the Hottentot and his burden to the surface without a pause, and when he had finished, Ralph's breathing was still even and quiet and there was not a single bead of perspiration on his face.

'So, Jan Cheroot, what did you find?'

Jan Cheroot was coated all over with fine pale dust through which his sweat had cut muddy runnels and he stank of bat guano and the mushroom odour of long-deserted caves. With hands that still shook with fear and exhaustion, he opened the flap of the saddle-bag at his waist.

'This is what I found,' he croaked, and Zouga took a lump of the raw rough rock from him.

It had a crystalline texture, that glittered like ice and was marbled with blue and riven by minute flaws and fissures, some of which had cracked through under the pounding of the iron adze with which Jan Cheroot had hacked it from the rock face. However, the shattered fragments of shining quartz were held together by the substance that had filled every crack and fault line in the ore. This cement was a thin malleable layer of bright metal, that twinkled in the sunlight when Zouga wet it with the tip of his tongue,

'By God, Ralph, will you look at that!' And Ralph took it from his father's hand with the reverence of a worshipper receiving the sacrament.

'Gold!' he whispered, and it sparkled at him, that lovely yellow smile that had captivated men almost from the time they had first stood upon their hindlegs.

'Gold!' Ralph repeated.

To find this glimmer of precious metal they had laboured most of their lives, father and son, they had ridden far and, in the company of other freebooters, had fought bloody battles, had helped destroy a proud nation and hunt a king to a lonely death.

Led by a sick man with swollen crippled heart and grandiose dreams, they had seized a vast land that now bore that giant's name, Rhodesia, and they had forced the land to yield up, one by one, its riches. They had taken its wide sweet pastures and lovely mountain ranges, its forests of fine native timber, its herds of sleek cattle, its legions of sturdy black men who for a pittance would provide the thews to gather in the vast harvest. And now at last they held the ultimate treasure in their hands.

'Gold!' Ralph said for the third time.

* * *

They struck their pegs along the ridge, cutting them from the living acacia trees that oozed clear sap from the axe cuts, and they hammered them into the hard earth with the flat of the blade. Then they built cairns of stone to mark the corner of each claim.

Under the Fort Victoria Agreement, which both of them had signed when they volunteered to ride against Lobengula's impis, they were each entitled to ten gold claims. This naturally did not apply to Jan Cheroot. Despite the fact that he had ridden into Matabeleland with Jameson's flying column and shot down the Matabele *amadoda* at the Shangani river and the Bembesi crossing with as much gusto as had his masters, yet he was a man of colour, and as such he could not share the spoils.

In addition to the booty to which Zouga and Ralph were entitled under the Victoria Agreement, both of them had bought up many blocks of claims from the dissolute and spendthrift troopers of Jameson's conquering force, some of whom had sold for the price of a bottle of whisky. So between them they could peg off the entire ridge and most of the valley bottoms on each side of it.

It was hard work, but urgent, for there were other prospectors abroad, one of whom could have followed their tracks. They worked through the heat of noon and by the light of the moon until sheer exhaustion forced them to drop their axes and sleep where they fell. On the fourth evening, they could stop at last, content that they had secured the entire reef for themselves. There was no gap between their pegs into which another prospector could jump.

'Jan Cheroot, there is only one bottle of whisky left,' Zouga groaned, and stretched his aching shoulders, 'but tonight I am going to let you pour your own dop.'

They watched with amusement the elaborate precautions which Jan Cheroot took to get the last drop into his brimming mug. In the process, the line around the bottom that marked his daily grog ration was entirely ignored, and when the mug was full, he did not trust the steadiness of his own hand but slurped up the first mouthful on all fours like a dog.

Ralph retrieved the bottle, and ruefully considered the remnants of the liquor before pouring a dram for his father and himself.

'The Harkness Mine,' Zouga gave them the toast.

'Why do you call it that?' Ralph demanded, when he lowered his mug and wiped his moustache with the back of his hand.

'Old Tom Harkness gave me the map that led me to it,' Zouga replied.

'We could find a better name.'

'Perhaps, but that's the one I want.'

'The gold will be just as bright, I expect,' Ralph capitulated, and carefully moved the whisky bottle out of the little Hottentot's reach, for Jan Cheroot had drained his mug already. 'I am glad we are doing something together again, Papa.' Ralph settled down luxuriously against his saddle.

'Yes,' Zouga agreed softly. 'It's been too long since we worked side by side in the diamond pit at New Rush.'

'I know just the right fellow to open up the workings for us. He is a top man, the best on the Witwatersrand goldfields, and I'll have my wagons bringing up the machinery before the rains break.'

It was part of their agreement that Ralph would provide the men and machinery and money to run the Harkness Mine when Zouga led him to it. For Ralph was a rich man. Some said he was already a millionaire, though Zouga knew that was unlikely. Nevertheless, Zouga remembered that Ralph had provided the transport and commissariat for both the Mashonaland column and the Matabeleland expedition against Lobengula, and for each he had been paid huge sums by Mr Rhodes' British South Africa Company, not in cash but in company shares. Like Zouga himself, he had speculated by buying up original land grants from the thriftless drifters that made up the bulk of the original column and had paid them in whisky, carried up from the railhead in his own wagons. Ralph's Rhodesia Lands Company owned more land than did even Zouga himself.

Ralph had also speculated in the shares of the British South Africa Company. In those heady days when the column first reached Fort Salisbury, he had sold shares that Mr Rhodes had issued to him

22

at £1 for the sum of £3-15s-0d on the London stock market. Then, when the pioneers' vaunting hopes and optimism had withered on the sour veld and barren ore bodies of Mashonaland, and Rhodes and Jameson were secretly planning their war against the Matabele king, Ralph had re-purchased British South Africans at eight shillings. He had then seen them quoted at £8 when the column rode into the burning ruins of Lobengula's kraal at GuBulawayo and the Company had added the entire realm of the Matabele monarch to its possessions.

Now, listening to his son talk with that infectious energy and charisma which even those hard days and nights of physical labour on the claims could not dull, Zouga reflected that Ralph had laid the telegraph lines from Kimberley to Fort Salisbury, that his construction gangs were at this moment laying the railway lines across the same wilderness towards Bulawayo, that his two hundred wagons carried trade goods to more than a hundred of Ralph's own trading-posts scattered across Bechuanaland and Matabeleland and Mashonaland, that as of today Ralph was a half-owner of a gold mine that promised to be as rich as any on the fabulous Witwatersrand.

Zouga smiled to himself as he listened to Ralph talk in the flickering firelight, and he thought suddenly, 'Damn it, but they might be right after all – the puppy might just possibly be a millionaire already.' And his pride was tinged with envy. Zouga himself had worked and dreamed from long before Ralph was born, had made sacrifice and had suffered hardships that still made him shudder when he thought about them, all for much lesser reward. Apart from this new reef, all he had to show for a lifetime of striving was King's Lynn and Louise – and then he smiled. With those two possessions, he was richer than Mr Rhodes would ever be.

Zouga sighed and tilted his hat forward over his eyes, and with Louise's beloved face held firmly in the eye of his mind he drifted into sleep, while across the fire Ralph still talked quietly, for himself more than for his father, and conjured up new visions of wealth and power.

*   *   *

It was two full days' ride back to the wagons, but they were still half a mile from the camp when they were spotted, and a joyous tide of servants and children and dogs and wives came clamouring out to greet them.

23

Ralph spurred forward and leaned low from the saddle to sweep Cathy up onto the pommel so violently that her hair tumbled into her face and she shrieked breathlessly until he silenced her with a kiss full on the mouth, and he held the kiss unashamedly while little Jonathan danced impatiently around the horse shouting, 'Me too! Lift me up, too, Papa!'

When at last he broke the kiss, Ralph held her close still, and his stiff dark moustaches tickled her ear as he whispered, 'The minute I get you into the tent, Katie my love, we will give that new mattress of yours a stiff test.'

She flushed a richer tone of pink and tried to slap his cheek, but the blow was light and loving. Ralph chuckled, then reached down and picked Jonathan up by one arm and dropped him into the gelding's croup behind the saddle.

The boy wrapped his arms around Ralph's waist and demanded in a high piping voice: 'Did you find gold, Papa?'

'A ton.'

'Did you shoot any lions?'

'A hundred.'

'Did you kill any Matabele?'

'The season's closed,' Ralph laughed, and ruffled his son's dark thick curls, but Cathy scolded quickly.

'That's a wicked thing to ask your father, you blood-thirsty little pagan.'

Louise followed the younger woman and the child at a more sedate pace, stepping lightly and lithely in the thick dust of the wagon road. Her hair was drawn back from her broad forehead and hung down her back to the level of her waist in a thick braid. It emphasized the high arches of her cheekbones.

Her eyes had changed colour again. It always fascinated Zouga to see the shifts of her mood reflected in those huge slanted eyes. Now they were a lighter softer blue, the colour of happiness. She stopped at the horse's head and Zouga stepped down from the stirrup and lifted the hat from his head, studying her gravely for a moment before he spoke.

'Even in such a short time I had forgotten how truly beautiful you are,' he said.

'It was not a short time,' she contradicted him. 'Every hour I am away from you is an eternity.'

It was an elaborate camp, for this was Cathy and Ralph's home. They owned no other, but like gypsies moved to where the pickings were richest. There were four wagons outspanned under the tall